to Jillian!

Good luck on the journey!

The North Star

Peter H. Reynolds

1999

The North Star

Written and Illustrated by
Peter H. Reynolds

FABLE VISION PRESS

The North Star

Published by
FableVision Press
44 Pleasant Street. Watertown, MA 02472

Second Printing 1999

ISBN 1-891405-01-2

Library of Congress Catalog Card no. 97-94615

Printed in Hong Kong

For more information: www.fablevision.com/northstar

dedicated
to all the parents
and teachers of the
w   o   r   l   d
and those who are
brave enough to
follow their
d   r   e   a   m s.

A
sweet
breeze met the
boy as he awoke
to his

journey.

He travelled on all fours
for quite sometime ...

And he grew.

And he paused.

One day he had the
urge to stand...
to walk.

It made his
journey easier...

He was soon
inspired to learn
how to run.

But for the most
Part he walked.

He wasn't afraid of
much.

He wandered the fields exploring, sometimes stopping

Sometimes going happily in circles... sometimes d a n c i n g .

Sometimes napping.

One day the boy saw
an oak leaf drift and
land on the water.

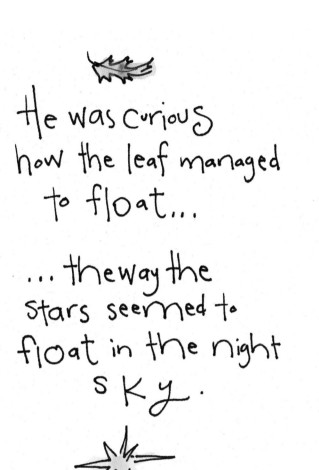

He was curious
how the leaf managed
to float...

... the way the
stars seemed to
float in the night
s k y .

A spray of sand
interrupted his thoughts.

"Where are you going
in such a hurry?"

But the rabbit
shot out of sight,
disappearing into a
path he had never
noticed before.

He left the
floating leaf and
wandered toward
the path...

...and there
he saw a cat.

The cat purrrred gently.

The boy asked...

"Where did the rabbit
go in such a hurry?"

"She was in a rush
to start her journey.
It's time for you to
start your
journey too."

The cat purrrred deeply.

"Oh, but I _have_ been on a journey! I've seen many wonderful things.

Some I understand and some I don't...

like how that leaf floats on the water..."

Well, that's fascinating, but I'd hate for you to be late.

You don't want to be

left

behind. "

"Behind? Who's
a head of me?"

"You wouldn't believe how many! You know, you're not the only one on this journey."

"Plenty ahead of you.
Lots to follow."

He began walking
down the path.

It stretched
out
far ahead
of him.

Signs kept pointing him along the way.

Some parts of the journey
were easy

and some were very difficult.

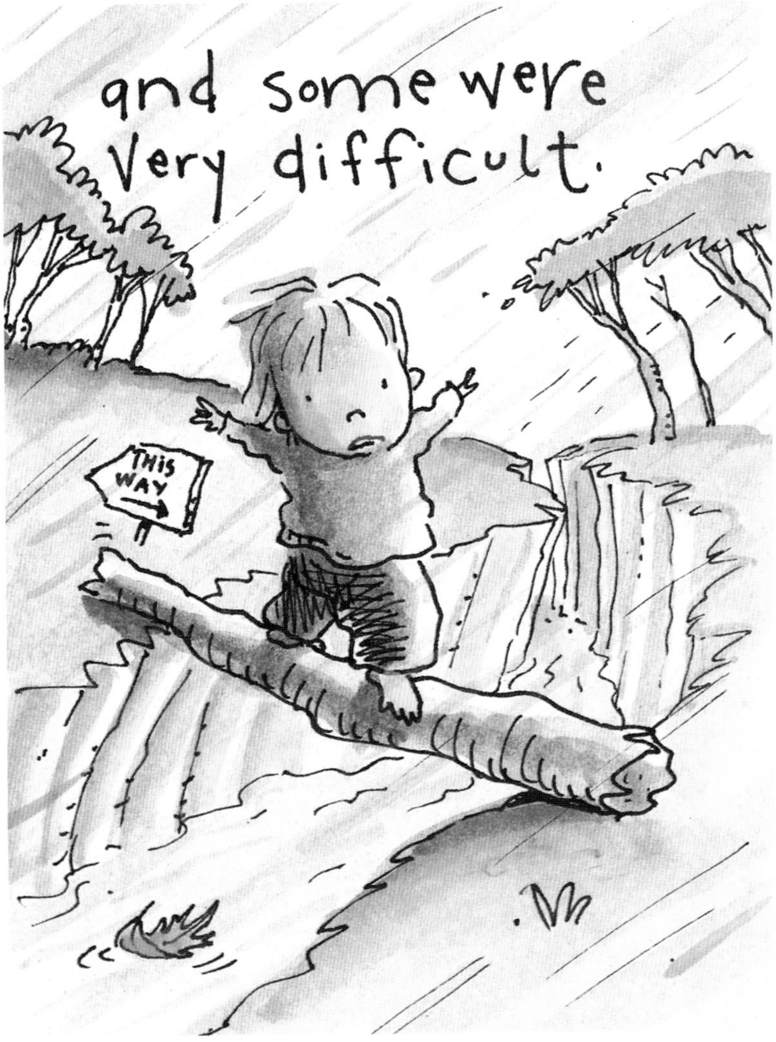

Although he
was following the
well-worn path,
he had a growing
feeling that he
was lost.

THIS
WAY

The forest
seemed to be
growing thicker
and the soil was
wet and muddy.

Clouds had
rolled in overhead
making everything
dark.

He rested...

... and noticed an oak leaf drift from the sky. It sailed with ease.

It swirled on a
breeze and
was carried
deep into the
forest ...

... it disappeared
behind a grove of trees.

The boy found
the leaf floating on
a pond in a peaceful
c l e a r i n g.

It looked like
a delicate boat
on a dreamy
voyage.

His gaze was
interrupted by
a voice...

"Oh! There you are!
I was worried! Don't
wander off like that!
Now Hurry. You're
falling behind!"

He ran... and ran... and ran... and as he ran he noticed the forest getting darker and thicker.
THIS WAY

The muddy ground became covered with water.
He could no longer see a clear path.

He sloshed through the swamp the best he could.

Until he
Came to a clearing
in the forest.
There he saw...

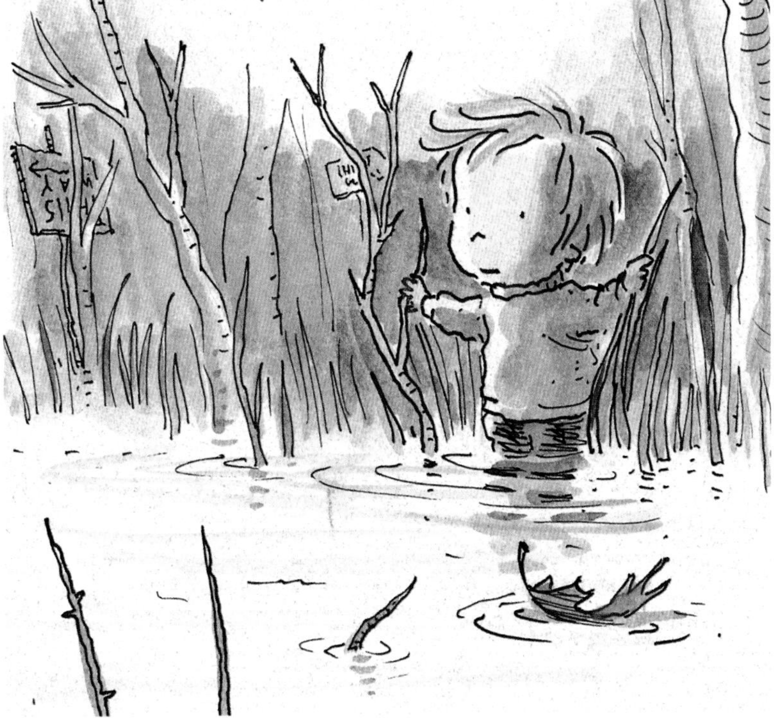

... a bjrd.

The boy marveled
at the bird's brilliant
feathers. He remembered
how he had once seen
a feather floating near
his beach.

I don't think so.
I mean, I'm not
sure if I'm lost. I
really hadn't thought
about it.'

"Hadn't thought about it? You must have some idea of where you are going, yes?"
"Well..."
THIS WAY

I've been
following
the path.

It seems like many people have taken it before me...

...and there have
been many signs
along the way...

And a
Very helpful
Cat guided me
back to the path
when I tried
to
wander.

the crickets fell
s i l e n t
as the bird asked...

"But where is
it that you
want to Be?"

I'm not sure, but I know this is not the place I want to be.

Ask yourself where
is it you want to go and
then follow the signs you
already know.

He was upset
that the bird
had flown away
into the cloudy
night sky.

He stared skyward
trying to see where
the bird had
gone.

And as he did
the clouds seemed to
melt... revealing the
inky black sky... and
there above him...

...was a
star,
a very
bright
star.

He stared at the star
and felt a whisper in
his ear, a pang in his heart,
a tingling in his spine.
He could hear the star.
The voice sounded so
f a m i l i a r .

He began to go in the direction of the star. Many other stars soon appeared in the dark velvet sky.

This WAY

All the stars
s t r e t c h e d
out above him, guiding
him like a great big
map as he navigated
out of the swamp.

THIS
WAY

He stopped and
rested a moment
and noticed something
appear in the stars.

His gaze was interrupted by
a deep voice coming from
behind him.

"What are you staring at?"
the voice croaked.

It was a frog.
"What is up there? What is so interesting?"

The boy waded closer
and answered, "Stars.
I'm looking at the stars."

"What stars?" The frog
was puzzled. "I see a
dark sky and mist and
low green clouds."

"You don't see them?"

"They are helping me guide myself out of this swamp."

"No thank you. I am quite at home here. I swam here as a tadpole and grew up here. Here I will stay."

The boy realized at
that moment that everyone
chas a different voyage,
different signs,

their own stars, their
own constellations.

The boy left
the frog who
was smiling
broadly.

Suddenly...
he heard a cry.
It was coming
from the center of the
deep river running
into the swamp.

It was the rabbit who had been in such a hurry.

She looked hungry and very tired.

The boy waded out
but realized the river
   was too deep.
The rabbit
was trapped.

He saw an oak leaf
drift by. It gave him
an idea.

The boy smiled having helped the rabbit on her own journey.

The boy looked
up and noticed
that the star
had become
even
b r i g h t e r.

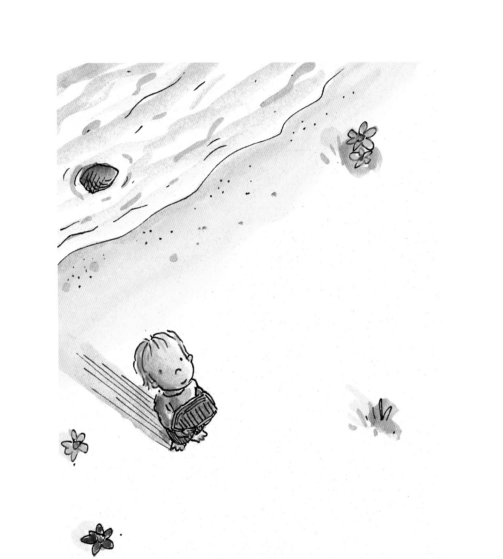

He followed the star and
as he did the muddy ground
grew drier... then grassy...
then soft and sandy.

Finally he came to a rest atop a dune and there below him was a beach...

. . . and a boat.

He gazed out
into the ocean
and he saw the
star.

The star glowed
patiently reminding
him that it was
still a long journey
ahead but it was
his own journey,
his very own
wonderful
journey.

The
Beginning